DISCOVER!

ANIMALS THAT SLITHER AND SLIDE

Legless Lizards

Enslow PUBLISHING

BY THERESA EMMINIZER

Please visit our website, www.enslow.com. For a free color catalog of all our high-quality books, call toll free 1-800-398-2504 or fax 1-877-980-4454.

Library of Congress Cataloging-in-Publication Data
Names: Emminizer, Theresa, author.
Title: Legless lizards / Theresa Emminizer.
Description: Buffalo : Enslow Publishing, [2024] | Series: Animals that slither and slide | Includes index. | Audience: Grades K-1
Identifiers: LCCN 2023029804 (print) | LCCN 2023029805 (ebook) | ISBN 9781978537323 (library binding) | ISBN 9781978537316 (paperback) | ISBN 9781978537330 (ebook)
Subjects: LCSH: Anniellidae–Juvenile literature. | Pygopodidae–Juvenile literature.
Classification: LCC QL666.L2256 E46 2024 (print) | LCC QL666.L2256 (ebook) | DDC 597.95/9-dc23/eng/20230712
LC record available at https://lccn.loc.gov/2023029804
LC ebook record available at https://lccn.loc.gov/2023029805

First Edition

Published in 2024 by
Enslow Publishing
2544 Clinton Street
Buffalo, NY 14224

Copyright © 2024 Enslow Publishing

Designer: Leslie Taylor
Editor: Theresa Emminizer

Photo credits: Cover (lizard) Ken Griffiths/Shutterstock.com, (slime background) AMarc/Shutterstock.com, (brush stroke) Sonic_S/Shutterstock.com, (slime frame) klyaksun/Shutterstock.com; Series Art (slime blob) Lemberg Vector studio/Shutterstock.com; p. 5 Ken Griffiths/Shutterstock.com; p.7 (snake) Yakov Oskanov/Shutterstock.com, (lizard) Ken Griffiths/Shutterstock.com; p.9 Clayton Lane/Shutterstock.com; p.11 COULANGES/Shutterstock.com; p.13 Jessicaluz/Shutterstock.com; p.15 Thomas Brown / https://commons.wikimedia.org/wiki/File:Slow_Worm_%28Anguis_fragilis%29_%286161776886%29.jpg; p.17 aaltair/Shutterstock.com; p.19 Ken Griffiths/Shutterstock.com; p.21 Dr.MYM/Shutterstock.com.

All rights reserved. No part of this book may be reproduced in any form without permission in writing from the publisher, except by a reviewer.

Some of the images in this book illustrate individuals who are models. The depictions do not imply actual situations or events.

Printed in the United States of America

CPSIA compliance information: Batch #CW24ENS: For further information contact Enslow Publishing, at 1-800-398-2504.

CONTENTS

What's That? 4

Not a Snake 6

Where Do They Live? 8

What Do They Eat? 10

Life of a Legless Lizard 12

Glass Lizards 14

Slowworms 16

Scaly-foot Lizards 18

Creepy or Cute? 20

Words to Know 22

For More Information 23

Index 24

Boldface words appear in
Words to Know.

WHAT'S THAT?

As their name suggests, legless lizards are lizards without legs! Some do have legs, but they're too small to walk on. Instead, legless lizards move by undulating, or moving their bodies in a wavelike way. Legless lizards are often mistaken for snakes or worms.

Legless lizards have smooth, scaly bodies.

NOT A SNAKE

What makes legless lizards different from snakes? Unlike snakes, lizards have moveable eyelids. They also have ears on the outside of their bodies. Snakes can expand, or widen, their **jaws**, but legless lizards can't. Snakes have forked (two-tipped) **tongues**, but legless lizards don't.

SNAKE

Do you think snakes and legless lizards look alike?

LEGLESS LIZARD

WHERE DO THEY LIVE?

Legless lizards can be found in North America, Europe, Asia, Australia, and Africa. Some like to live in loose soil, leaves, or grass. Others are found in sandy **habitats**. Legless lizards like to hide underneath boards, roots, or rocks.

There are many different species, or kinds, of legless lizards.

WHAT DO THEY EAT?

What a legless lizard eats depends on where it lives. Most eat bugs and other **invertebrates**. Legless lizards hunt during the day and at night. They have strong teeth and jaws to help them catch and eat food.

Legless lizards help keep bug populations in check.

LIFE OF A LEGLESS LIZARD

Female legless lizards lay eggs. A group of eggs is called a clutch. There are usually around 5 to 10 eggs in a clutch. The mother stays with her eggs to keep them safe until they **hatch**.

Here, a legless lizard rests by her egg.

GLASS LIZARDS

Glass lizards are legless lizards that grow to be about 43 inches (108 cm) long. They're usually light brown or yellow colored. Glass lizards got their name because their tails can easily break off! This happens when they are scared or caught by a predator. It can help the lizard get away!

After a glass lizard's tail breaks, it can slowly grow back.

15

SLOWWORMS

Slowworms are legless lizards found in grassy or wooded places in Europe. Slowworms can be almost 20 inches (50 cm) long. Females are usually bigger than males. Most slowworms have a golden grey color. They can live upwards of 50 years!

Slowworms are sometimes called blindworms because their eyes are so small!

17

SCALY-FOOT LIZARDS

Scaly-foot lizards are around 5 inches (12 cm) long. They live in the forests and on the coasts of Australia. Scaly-foot lizards got their name because they have small, scaly flaps near their tail that look almost like feet!

Here, a scaly-foot lizard **basks** in the sun.

19

CREEPY OR CUTE?

Legless lizards might look a little odd, but don't be scared! These slithery animals don't usually harm people. In fact, they're very helpful. Gardeners can thank legless lizards for keeping the populations of garden pests such as slugs in check. They may not be cute, but they're certainly useful!

WORDS TO KNOW

bask: To rest in the sun in order to get warmer.

habitat: The natural place where an animal or plant lives.

hatch: To break open or come out of.

invertebrate: An animal without a backbone.

jaw: The bones that hold the teeth and make up the mouth.

population: The number of animals of the same kind that live in a place.

tongue: The soft, movable part of the mouth that is used for tasting and eating food, and that humans use for speaking.

FOR MORE INFORMATION

BOOKS

Gottlieb, Beth. *I Love Lizards!* New York, NY: Gareth Stevens Publishing, 2023.

Hughes, Sloane. *20 Things You Didn't Know About Reptile Adaptations.* New York, NY: Rosen Publishing, 2023.

WEBSITES

Slowworms: Britannica
www.britannica.com/animal/slowworm
Learn more about slowworms and how they live!

Smithsonian's National Zoo
nationalzoo.si.edu/animals/news/stripy-slithery-splendid-european-glass-lizard-hatchlings
Read a fun story about hatching glass lizards!

Publisher's note to educators and parents: Our editors have carefully reviewed these websites to ensure that they are suitable for students. Many websites change frequently, however, and we cannot guarantee that a site's future contents will continue to meet our high standards of quality and educational value. Be advised that students should be closely supervised whenever they access the internet.

INDEX

Africa, 8

Asia, 8

Australia, 8, 18

body, 4, 5, 6, 10, 14, 15, 18

color, 14, 16

eggs, 12

Europe, 8, 16

food, 10

habitat, 8

kinds, 9, 14, 16, 18

North America, 8

pet, 21

snakes, 4, 6, 7

undulating, 4